Published in the United States of America by Crown Publishers, Inc.,
225 Park Avenue South, New York, New York 10003
Published in Great Britain by Walker Books, Ltd.,
184-192 Drummond Street, London NW1 3HP
CROWN, IT'S GREAT TO READ!, and logo are trademarks of Crown Publishers, Inc.
Manufactured in Italy.

Library of Congress Cataloging-in-Publication Data
Baynton, Martin. Fifty gets the picture. (It's great to read!) Summary: Fifty the tractor
gives the farm hand Wally some assistance in his chores so that he will have the
time to finish painting Fifty's portrait. [1. Tractors—Fiction.   2. Farm life—Fiction.
3. Painting—Fiction]   I. Title.   II. Series.
PZ7.B347Fh   1986   [E]   86-6352
ISBN 0-517-56355-X

10 9 8 7 6 5 4 3 2 1   First American Edition

FIFTY
GETS
THE PICTURE

Martin Baynton

CROWN PUBLISHERS, INC., NEW YORK

It was Wally's day off and he was painting Fifty's portrait. Fifty looked very smart. Everything was fine until the farmer came along.

"Sorry, Wally," he said, "you must work after all. There's rain on the way."

Fifty was disappointed. He was looking forward to seeing his portrait.

But there was plowing to be done while the ground was still dry. Fifty had to make the best of it.

Wally was daydreaming, as usual, so Fifty steered himself. He kept a sharp eye out for the moles who popped up to say hello. Fifty always spotted them and always drove around them.

But what a mess it made of the neat
plow-lines!

When the farmer saw his field he
was upset.

"I want straight lines, not molehills,"
he grumbled.

Wally's next job was a long one. The
gateway at the top of the lane was
always flooding. The farmer was fed up
with it. He told Wally to put a drain
under it—before the next downpour.

When Wally went off for lunch, Fifty woke his friend Norris the rat.

"Let's finish the job," he said. "Then Wally can finish his painting."

"How can we?" Norris asked.

"With the help of the moles," Fifty replied.

Fifty asked the moles to dig a tunnel under the gateway. The moles were glad to help and burrowed furiously.

Then Norris and the moles ran a
tow rope through the tunnel and tied it
to Fifty.

"Good work, everyone," said Fifty.
"Now tie the rope to the pipe and
stand back!"

Fifty started his engine and pulled. His huge wheels spun in the muddy ditch. He chose another gear and tried again. This time his wheels held firm and he dragged the pipe into the tunnel.

When Wally came back he was delighted. But he wasn't surprised. Nothing about Fifty ever surprised him.

At last he could finish the portrait. But just as he started . . . *Boom!* A cloud burst and rain fell in torrents.

"Oh dear," said the farmer, looking at Wally's ruined painting. "Too bad. But I see you've already done one portrait today!"

.He pointed up at the field where Fifty had plowed around all the moles.

What a picture!

Wally laughed and patted Fifty on the hood.

"Well done, pal," he whispered.

Fifty pretended to be surprised, but he couldn't hide the smile on his face.